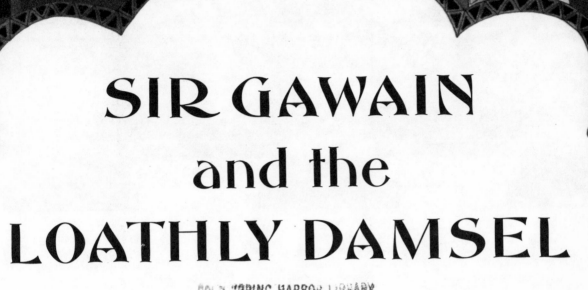

SIR GAWAIN
and the
LOATHLY DAMSEL

Retold and illustrated by
JOANNA TROUGHTON

E. P. DUTTON & CO., INC. NEW YORK

SBN: 0-525-39380-3   LCC: 70-186297

Printed in Great Britain
First Edition

Long, long ago there lived a king
called Arthur who was ruler of all
Britain. He had many brave knights,
but perhaps the bravest, and the one
that Arthur loved best, was his
nephew, Sir Gawain.

It happened one day when Arthur and his knights were holding a feast at Carlisle that into the feasting hall rode a sorrowing lady on a white palfrey. "My lord Arthur," she cried, "Help me I beg of you. My name is Lady Mordron. My husband has been captured by the Black Knight of Tarn Wathelyne. This evil knight has boasted that not even King Arthur himself dares to do battle with him. I plead that you take up his challenge."

Upon hearing these words, Arthur declared that he would ride out at once to the Castle of Tarn Wathelyne, and he ordered his horse and weapons be made ready. Gawain begged to go in Arthur's place, for it was, indeed, a dangerous quest. But the king was decided. Finally, however, King Arthur agreed that Gawain should ride with him, but only for part of the way.

So Arthur and Gawain followed Lady Mordron out of Carlisle and into the great dark forest of Inglewood. After they had travelled some miles, Arthur bade Gawain to follow him no further but to wait until he returned, and the king and Lady Mordron rode deeper into the forest.

At length they came to a clearing, and there before him
Arthur saw a black and foul-smelling lake on which
stood a grim castle. On the drawbridge of the castle,
mounted on a coal-black horse, was Gromer Somer
Joure, the Black Knight of Tarn Wathelyne.

"Fight me if you dare,
King Arthur of Britain!"
shouted Gromer Somer Joure.

"That I will," replied King Arthur. He set his spear and urged his horse into a gallop down the slope, but all the while he failed to notice the evil smile which crossed the face of Lady Mordron.

As Arthur reached the drawbridge, his horse reared up in terror, and a fear as cold as ice swept over the king. "What vile magic is this?" he cried in alarm.

"It is the magic of my mistress, Lady Mordron," sneered Gromer Somer Joure. "She led you into this trap. She wishes to be ruler of all Britain in your place. But I will give you one chance before I slay you," he continued. "If you meet me here in a year and a day with the answer to this riddle: What is it in all the world that women most desire? I will spare you your life!"

Arthur made his way back to where Gawain was waiting, and told his nephew all that had passed. And so it was that they rode out together for a year and a day, to discover what women most desire in all the world. Some said, "Idleness", and others, "Beauty".

Some said, "Riches", and others, "A fine husband". But Arthur and Gawain felt in their hearts that none of these answers would satisfy Gromer Somer Joure.

When the appointed time came they journeyed once more to the Castle of Tarn Wathelyne.

They were passing through Inglewood when a figure
appeared in the distance. As King Arthur and Gawain
drew nearer they saw it was a damsel. But . . .

She was the loathliest damsel that ever walked the earth!

"Think twice before you pass me by, good knights,"
she cackled, "for I know of your quest, and I can tell you
the answer that you seek. But in return the fair Sir
Gawain must promise to marry me." Gawain turned pale
with horror, and Arthur begged him to refuse. But, to
save the king's life, Gawain willingly made the promise.
And the loathly damsel told Arthur the answer to the
riddle.

When the king reached Tarn Wathelyne, the Black Knight was waiting on the drawbridge as before, and at a window of the castle was the face of the evil Lady Mordron. Arthur reined up his horse and cried with a great shout: "Here is your answer, Gromer Somer Joure—what women most desire in all the world is to rule over men!" A piercing scream of rage came from Lady Mordron, and Gromer Somer Joure turned and galloped back into the castle.

Around the lake a thick mist sprang up.

When the mist cleared, the castle was nowhere to be seen. Only a green lake was left, filled with sweet-smelling water-flowers. So Arthur, Gawain and the Loathly Damsel returned to Carlisle, there to prepare for the wedding.

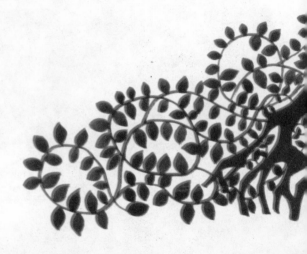

The very next day Sir Gawain and the Loathly Damsel were married. People ran into the streets to cheer the bride and groom, but their cheers turned into wails once they saw the hideous creature that rode by Gawain's side.

When the wedding feast was over the married couple retired to their private chambers. "Come sweet husband," croaked the Loathly Damsel. "Give your wife a kiss."

And Gawain overcome by a sudden pity bent
down and kissed his ugly bride.

When Gawain raised his head, he saw before him the most beautiful damsel in all the world. "Where is my wife?" he gasped. "I am your wife," she answered. "My name is Lady Ragnall. With that kiss you have broken part of the spell put upon me by my jealous sister, Lady Mordron, who all her life has feared me as a rival. It was her magic that made me so loathly. But you must now choose, whether you wish me to be loathly by day when all the world can see me, or by night when we are alone together. Beautiful by day, or beautiful by night." Gawain, seeing the sadness in her eyes, replied at once: "It is you who will suffer most, my lady, so let the choice be yours."

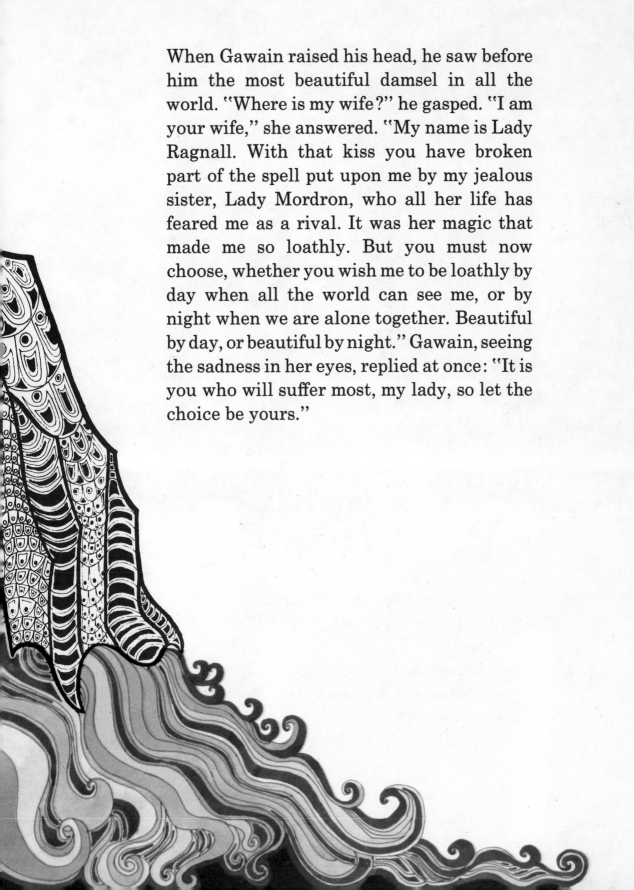

Upon these words, Lady Ragnall cried out in joy: "Oh Gawain, because you left the choice to me, the spell is now completely broken, and I can be beautiful at all times. My evil sister told me that only a true knight could banish this magic. She swore that I would never find such a man, but that man is you, my husband." And Sir Gawain and the Lady Ragnall lived in great happiness ever after.